BOTH
PUBLISHING

Published in 2023 by BOTH Publishing

The author asserts their moral right to be identified as the author of their work, in accordance with the Copyright, Designs and Patents Act, 1988.

A CIP catalogue record of this book is available from the British Library

ISBN - 978-1-913603-29-8

Paperback available
ISBN - 978-1-913603-30-4

Distributed by BOTH Publishing.

Cover design by Alistair Sims and Chrissey Harrison. Cover illustrations by Cattallina, licensed via Shutterstock.
Typeset by Chrissey Harrison.

Part of the Dyslexic Friendly Quick Reads Series.

www.booksonthehill.co.uk

THE DUST OF THE RED ROSE KNIGHT

James Bennett

Other dyslexic friendly quick read titles from BOTH publishing

Silver for Silence

Sharpe's Skirmish

Six Lights off Green Scar

Blood Toll

The Clockwork Eyeball

Anchor Point

At Midnight I Will Steal Your Soul

The House on the Old Cliffs

Sherlock Holmes and the
Four Kings of Sweden

The Man Who Would Be King

Foreword

By Peter James

Back in 2010 I wrote my first *Quick Reads* novella, *THE PERFECT MURDER*. This was written as adult fiction but with no long words, and was aimed at people who struggled in some way with literacy.

I was lucky enough to win the *Reader's Favourite Award*. At the reception, I was approached by a lady in her late 50s who was close to tears. She told me my novella was the first book she had ever read that was not written for children. For years she had been too embarrassed ever to read in public – on a beach, a park or a bus or a train – because the only stories she was able to cope with were children's books.

Looking at the dyslexic friendly books BOTH published last year I can see how the larger spacing between the words and larger print create an easy-to-read and accessible format without detracting from the narrative journey. I am excited to be part of their project as it is thanks to initiatives such as the work BOTH is doing, that the condition of dyslexia is now catered for in fiction, and people, such as the lady I met, can hold her head up and read in public, like so many other ordinary people.

The Dust

of the

Red Rose

Knight

This one is for Liz Smith.

So short you might read it.

Only fools want to be great.

The Once and Future King

T.H. White

I

In which Tomas, our hero, learns that he is pursued.

It befell in the days of Arthur Pendragon, when he was king of all England, and so reigned, that there lived a thief and a lover of men called Tomas, the Red Rose Knight. You won't find this tale in the Matter of Britain nor in the *Historia Brittonum,* the earliest Arthurian text. By the time the Victorian era rolled around, Tomas had all but vanished completely – *poof!* – along with all his galivanting, not to mention the gay diversions in which he so loved to delight. And which saw him expunged from the annals of myth and legend. No Parsifal, he.

But long ago, when the walls of Camelot shone above the treetops of Broceliande (and before a certain wizard got trapped in an oak that is sometimes a tower of glass and sometimes a talkative sword) Tomas was said to dwell deep in the forest, among the roses and thorns. The son of a shepherd and (so they said) a fairy, Tomas was born as wild as the briar beneath his boots, of which his blood made him a part. Following his father's death months previous, the lad had made a living as an outlaw on the king's roads, relieving this or that duchess of gold, rubies, diamonds and pearls.

This, in case you hadn't guessed, is his story.

How he rode, our errant knight, our fabled far-from-champion in his red leather armour, his billowing cloak and cap. Raven haired, spark-eyed and fit as a royal whippet he was. Tireless in the saddle and long in the scabbard, or so his conquests claimed, who stretched from the snowy kingdom of Lodainn to the cloudy borders of Lyonesse. This morning, Tomas had been up on the Giant's Knoll on the northernmost edge of the forest, gazing, as was his wont, at the distant towers that looked like pillars holding up the sun, or swords plucked from lakes, gleaming with destiny. Camelot always tugged at his breast in a way he'd never been able to place, not for all the books he'd read or all his adventures. It was a curdling of longing and resentment, topped by the cherry of a nameless shame.

The sight brought to mind, as it always did, the counsel of his poor dead father.

"Mourn not the place that God has given you," the old man would say, herding his pigs and ploughing his meagre vegetable patch. He was a religious man and philosophical with it. "Camelot is home to the purest of knights, who have sworn themselves to the king's code, to serve the weak and the helpless, to give succour to widows and suchlike. Envy them not, for God has placed them higher for a reason."

Tomas, who'd seen plenty of knights

6

for himself, tended to curl his lip.

"Aye, brave indeed," he'd reply, or words to that effect. "Availing themselves of the thanks of lady and spinner alike, in coins, kisses and more."

The old shepherd would chuckle, but at folly rather than in mirth.

"Those of the Table Round would touch the wingtips of angels themselves. Ah, but you're a bitter seed, Tomas. Remember your place does not forestall your right to climb."

The old man had died as all mortals must and Tomas had learnt to keep his thoughts to himself. To hell with Arthur and all of his knights! Tomas was his own creature and subject to none. In the armour his mother had given him, an heirloom of crimson leather, fine embroidery and a macaw-feathered cap, the self-styled 'Red Rose Knight' lived by his wits alone. That being the lifting of gold from the king's carriages, trickery, gambling and carousing. And among other things, the swiving of prince, prelate and pauper from the northern edge of Broceliande to the bounds of its darkling heart. Why should he, so far from Camelot and lofty ideals, go without comfort and sport?

On this day, Tomas wheeled his horse, a russet roan called Jorget, from the vexing sight of the castle and thundered into the south. Well he made haste, for he had spied from his lookout the fact that he was pursued. And by a knight! A strange rider all in blue armour, enamelled and inlaid with pearl, who sported a lance and a peafowl feather plume. Tomas had spied the man on a bridge and at a crossroads. An hour ago, the knight had called out to him through the trees, asking to parley and confirming the fact that Tomas was indeed the one he sought.

"Hold now, in Arthur's name! Hold, good sir, and heed my enquiry."

Tomas rode on.

Come dusk, he was tiring, the knight still at his back. The Blue Knight, as it happened, had drawn near enough to hail him with the horn around his neck, all twinkling with ivory and gold. As its sounding rang between the trees (a musical sound, like a courting wolf or a bourdon bell) Tomas found that Jorget wouldn't budge, the horse tossing his head and snorting, his hooves planted firmly in the mud. Face as red as his cap, Tomas turned in the saddle and demanded of the man the cause of his doggedness. The Blue Knight would pay for this insult. Come to think of it, he might have jewels in his pouch.

"I am Sir Persant of Inde," Sir Persant of Inde said, breathless and scowling, his visor up. "A knight of the Table Round. Tell me, do you always flee from strangers so? According to Arthur's code, all must obey those in authority. Why, your scarpering smacks of villainy! Slip me again and there isn't a leaf in this greenwood that'll hide you."

"All of you knights do prattle so," Tomas retorted, his sword unsheathed. He trembled a little; Persant bore the mien of a Persian prince with his rich brown skin, strong jaw and most notably, his muscular arms. And he was encased in steel. "What reason have I to trust you?"

"Sir," Persant replied, "I swear by the Alicorn around my neck, carved as it was from a unicorn, that I am true. The king sent me forth to seek out one called Tomas, the Red Rose Knight, and on finding him to bring him to court."

Aha! thought Tomas. *My fame precedes me. It seems I've lifted a coin too many from the royal carriages.* Then he pulled a face. *Arthur, the old bedswerver!* He thought this last because

11

his father, the shepherd, had told him it was so. Behind the curtain of chivalry, Anton O' Lincoln had claimed that the Bear King liked to have his way with any willing duchess, damsel or dame, and that was why the realm was descending into chaos. *Who in Logres has cause to obey him?*

"Tomas who?" said Tomas. Yet the invitation – the threat – stirred the awe in him. A journey to Camelot!

Yet only on my own terms, thought he. *And never so readily.*

"You look suitably red to me, sir," Persant replied. "In your crimson leather, fine embroidery and macaw-feathered cap."

To the Blue Knight, Tomas said, "This

forest is vast and filled with all manner of perils." He smiled, his eyes resting on the prize around the knight's neck, the horn all gilded and white against his fancy armour. "If the ogres don't get you, the bewitchments and noxious fogs shall. The heart of Broceliande is dark and ruled by the Archimago, a warlock if ever there was one. Away with you now. I know of no such knight! Away!"

Persant did not away. A clash ensued, which soon ended up with both knights dismounted, blade to tempered blade. As the sun set and the forest grew dim, the both of them grew bored and agreed to a truce – at least until the break of dawn. In this spirit, Persant built a fire and Tomas snared a deer. After supping venison and wine, and a pulling off of boots and armour, a different kind of jousting commenced, one of wit and flirtation – for Tomas had an eye for diversion, as has been told. Moreover, the forest was lonesome. And knights in those days were *knights,* you understand, with bold words and scant reservation when it came to damsels or, in this case, damoiseaux.

Blood high, Tomas spoke in admiration of the Blue Knight's horn, which indeed had once belonged to a unicorn and which he'd procured in a game of dice in distant Ctesiphon. The horn held the power of 'beastly summoning', he went on, calling any beast who heard it to the bearer's aid, an advantage in a forest as boundless as Broceliande. It explained why Jorget had stalled at its sounding.

"Come morn," Tomas told the knight, "I shall point you to the Fairy Fountain where dwells the Red Rose Knight. You might catch the bastard unawares and drag him to King Arthur's court."

Then Tomas was rubbing at the surprised Persant, until his girth swelled to match his pride and the Red Rose Knight unleashed a different kind of lance from his breeches. Soon enough, Tomas did show the Blue Knight the bud for which he was named and proceeded to ride his pursuer as though galloping from the Gates of Hell. A tangle of Saxon and Saracen limbs, Tomas and Persant swived merrily in the glade until midnight, the branches ringing overhead with their cries.

Before he slept, drunk and dazed, the Blue Knight enquired, "Sweet knave, how come you know where the rogue dwell? I thought you knew naught of the Red Rose Knight?"

It was then that a fox passed that way and spying them by the fire said, "Never trust one of fay-blood! And twice over if his name be Tomas!"

Tomas hissed at the beast, but it was pointless. The Blue Knight, sated, was fast asleep and snoring.

In the morning, Persant found his boots, his pouch and the Alicorn gone, left in the dust of the Red Rose Knight.

II

In which Tomas comes to the Fairy Fountain and encounters an enchantress.

Tomas galloped into the morning wood. No knight of the Table would ever catch him! Fleet as the wind, his horse thundered down myriad paths, passing under crooked oaks and bent willows, over rushing creeks and through thorny briars. *'Arse!'* a hare cried as it leapt from his path, but Tomas's blood was in his ears and he didn't hear it. With the stolen horn jouncing at his breast, Tomas raced over the Forbidden Hill where the squat Castle Corbenic floated, its haunted towers roaming through the mist. Come midday, he reached the shore of the Lake Perilous where no man or woman (or anyone for that matter) should gaze at their reflection lest they find themselves trapped under its surface and where only the pure of heart could traverse the waters on the back of awaiting swans.

Tomas went around.

Come dusk, he'd cut his way through the snares of the Cob Queen who lurked in those parts, crept with cap over nose through a noxious fog and then on and on, over the Blasted Heath where the giants roamed, their howls sonorous in the brume, their boots shaking the earth. In the shadow of their dangling balls, Tomas swept into the woods and came at last to the Clearing of the Fairy Fountain where he leapt off his horse.

"You're welcome," Jorget snarked, but Tomas ignored her.

Taking a cup from his cloak (a goblet he'd filched from a merchant on his way to a Camelot fair), Tomas knelt on the steps of the ancient spring and took a sip of the crystal-clear waters. Many searched far and wide for the fountain, over dale and under hill. And why not? For the fountain promised Eternal Youth. Had he been entirely mortal, the Red Rose Knight might've danced a jig. But his blood was laced with that of the Fay, which kept him spry and granted him an ear for the beasts, not that he thought it much of a gift. The fountain could only cool him.

"Mother," he spoke into the waters. "Come hence, dear, and answer me. Why does the Blue Knight seek me in the woods? How has the king come to learn of me? Am I to pay for my crimes?"

"'Twas a letter from the blasted shepherd," the Enchantress Hellawes said, who appeared in the reflections in the bowl of the fountain, her face in a scowl and her pointy ears aquiver. "It was Anton's last wish, sent to the king upon his expiry. For months, the king must've pondered it. Why anyone would honour Arthur, with all his lecherous ways, is beyond me. Ah, but it's good to see you, my son."

"And you, Mother," said Tomas. "But this enlightens me naught."

"Then know that not one knight hunts

you," said she of the Isle of Apples (and of late the Wood Ensorcelled, though 'of late' to Hellawes was a thousand years and you'd think her no older than the knave who knelt before her.) "But three. Come find me in the Fortress Impenetrable, deep in the heartwood. There you shall learn a Truth Most Vital. Fear not! No king, no Pin-dick-dragon, shall steal my get from me!"

Tomas sucked his teeth, for his mother, he knew, had never quite taken to the courtly tongue.

"And what," he ventured, "of the Archimago who lurks in those parts? Spry I am, and cunning. A warlock the equal of Merlin I have no desire to face."

"The Archimago and I have come to a… mutual accord."

"And how, pray tell, shall I get there?"

"Why, 'tis simple." The Enchantress Hellawes who'd crossed gulfs of infinite void to reach the earthly realm and lingered, causing all manner of misdeeds and complications, said. "Make your way through the Singing Marsh and be mindful not to set one boot on the grass lest the boggarts devour you. Skirt the Mournful Mound and watch out for the Wyrm of the Barrow. Cross the Amorous Ford yet drink of it not lest an unsought passion befall you. At the Narrow Mountain, high in a cave, seek out an old and forgetful woman called Duessa Le Feu. Besides myself, she alone knows the way to the Fortress Impenetrable, that is sometimes called the Castle of Tears or the Castle of the Most Ill Adventure or the Castle Without A Name."

Tomas, the Red Rose Knight, sighed.

"Mother, that doesn't sound simple."

But the fountain was still. The Enchantress was gone.

III

In which Tomas makes his way to the mountains and wakes up to a sword at his throat.

'A Truth Most Vital', his mother had said. What in God's name could it mean? Wild as he was, Tomas was no fool. The Blue Knight had taught him naught, apart from the fact that codes were made of words alone and guile was a good way to lighten a man's pocket. Over the years, he'd seen Hellawes get up to all manner of tricks, from setting the Knights of the Table Round impossible (and deadly) tasks to ensorcelling travellers from faraway lands. And now she was in league with the Archimago whose reach extended deep into Broceliande where presumably the Fortress Impenetrable clawed at the sky with bats flapping around its turrets and screams resounding from the dungeons under it.

No one was perfect. Hellawes was his mother and he loved her. That aside, it was plain that all wasn't quite as it seemed. As a youth, with hay in his hair and holes in his breeches, he'd often thought himself a character in a book and that Time was bound at either end, much like a tale told. If only one could go skipping through the pages, one might learn of the future! When he closed his eyes, he seemed to see ramparts and a black robed man, swords raised and fire in the sky... It was too vague to tell whether his blood granted him a sliver of the sight or whether he was dreaming.

The Red Rose Knight found himself bewildered. Why were *three* knights on his heels? And come to think of it, why had Hellawes chosen to bed with Anton O'Lincoln in the first place, who was but a lowly pig herder? What letter had the old man sent to the king – Arthur of all people! – and what did it say? Had he expressed the same disappointment he'd expressed to Tomas (and that the peasants thereabouts liked to say had been the death of him), the shame of his son's business in the forest, his wantonness and thievery? Why, oh why, did it have to be today when his spirits were high, the greenwood endless and coffers of gold likely to rattle down the road at any moment?

Instead, he found himself saddled with a quest. If he'd wanted quests, he'd have gone to Camelot and knelt before the king like so many other young fools, begging for adventure, nights in the rain and thorns in his backside. Down the winding track went Tomas. Through the Singing Marsh he rode where to set one boot upon the sward was to tempt the boggarts who lurked there. The midges had no appetite for fairy blood and he was merely weary when he cantered into the shadow of the Mournful Mound.

There were many myths surrounding the Mound, each one bloodier than the last, and Tomas was wary, particularly of the wyrm. In great charred ditches and spirals of earth, the hill rose, marking the eastern edge of the forest. Beyond, the Narrow Mountain loomed, wyverns flying around its peak and trolls in every crevice, or so Tomas presumed. Where the trees gave way to the foot of the slope Tomas leapt off his horse and made camp. Tonight he wouldn't risk a fire – this place had seen enough of it, he thought – satisfying himself with a rind of cheese pilfered from a farmer three days ago.

Before he fell into restless dreams, a grizzled badger passed that way and muttered at the knight.

"Obey the king and get thee to court. Would you refuse your destiny?"

"Oh, fuck off," Tomas said and slept.

Come morning, he woke up to a sword at his throat.

IV

In which – shit! Dragon!

Oof! Tomas ducked another swing of the Black Knight's mace and went staggering up the slope. He was painfully aware of the cliff at his back and the waterfall roaring in his ears. This was where the river crashed down over the rocks and flowed for a mile or so to the Amorous Ford, the legendary waters swirling under an old bridge, a speck in the distance. Tomas would rather not swirl with it, the spray all around him, but his foe was gaining ground.

The Black Knight was taller than any knight Tomas had seen (and he'd seen the Green Knight once, off in the trees, a spindle of branches and leaves). The feather in his cap weaved in the shadow of the man's shoulders and had done so since Tomas had awakened and kicked the knight's legs out from under him, rolling away in the thicket and scrabbling for his sword.

Around and around the Mournful Mound the two of them duelled. Jorget had whinnied and scarpered – so much for escape on horseback. Tomas might've claimed he was someone else, just as he'd done with Sir Persant, but the horn around his neck had betrayed him. In armour the colour of doom, his dark plume swishing, the Black Knight did all in his power to make Tomas yield, grunting with the ascent.

"Submit, Red Rose Knight," the Black Knight said, his growls amplified by his helmet, an ornate horror of grille and wings. "For I am charged by the king himself. I, Oriols of Lis, who sailed from that strange and ferocious land, and has slain a thousand felons and more. Would you leap to your death?"

"I might," Tomas said, daring a glance at the drop behind him, "and let fate and the waters decide."

It was a long way down and the river fierce. He'd prefer to avoid both if he could.

"Even so, best me you cannot. For I wear the Helm Volitant. In my plume there are two golden feathers, each plucked from a griffin and each affording the power of flight. Why, the third of the feathers brought me hence, sailing over the treetops. Leap and I shall pluck you from the river."

On the precipice, Tomas cocked his head, his ears atwitch. Much like the Alicorn around his neck, a helm that might bear him up the Narrow Mountain and away from this place would prove most useful.

"Must've been a long flight from Camelot, sir, simply to apprehend a knave."

The Black Knight, as knights were wont to do, was prattling again.

"Fear not, briar knight. I am one who heeds the code," said Oriols. "To persevere to the end of any enterprise, and so you shall not escape me. I come to see you to court and nothing more, with your head safe upon your shoulders. Yield! Refrain from this pointless fray."

"Pointless to you, perchance," Tomas replied. "Tell me, Oriols of Lis, why do knights hunt me in the forest?"

Oriols shook his mace, guffawing.

"Nay. You'll hear it from the king or none. That was the oath I swore."

With this, the Black Knight lashed out again. It might've been the vanquishing blow if not for a trembling of the earth that threw both knights off their feet. It was then a section of the Mound shuddered and snorted. What they'd thought rocks slithered and uncoiled, shaking off ash to reveal scales of golden red beneath. *The Wyrm of the Barrow!* Wings eclipsed the sun, the light through them dousing the hillside in blood. A snout, many horned and studded with fangs, arose from the whirling dust.

"Shit! *Dragon!*" cried Oriols. Though it was far from advisable, he snapped up his visor to get a better look. Tomas followed his gaze, finding himself dwarfed by eyes larger than a house. They shone a deep crimson he couldn't help but admire, if not the fury inside them.

"Shit!" Tomas echoed. There was no other word for it; Oriols and himself were exposed on the hillside. Under the circumstances, the sword he held was no better than a needle.

"Shit!" shrieked a goat as it galloped past them down the slope, followed by a herd of sheep, all bleating and afeard.

Winded as he was, Tomas had lost none of his wits. He fumbled for the Alicorn around his neck, remembering the Blue Knight's claim and meaning to summon some beast thereabouts to come to his aid... Before he could sound the horn, the Black Knight was before him, pulling him to his feet.

"And now, knave, we have common cause."

"To fight a dragon?"

"No. To flee."

So saying, Oriols shoved Tomas down the slope in a shower of scree. There was a reason why knights lived to tell of such beasts (exaggerated as the tales were) and I suppose you would've done the same. The Red Rose Knight went tumbling head over heels, rolling with his foe through the ash and bones of the Mournful Mound as the world filled up with flame.

Later, singed and exhausted, the Red Rose Knight and the Black shared bowls of boiled trout around a campfire. A truce had been declared, at least until dawn. It was raining and the two of them sat under the boughs by the river on the charred eastern edge of Broceliande. The dragon had made a couple of sweeps and roared off over the treetops, loath to reduce the canopy to cinders. In those days, the forest was under the protection of Arthur – and watched over by others besides – and there were laws about such things. Even a dragon knew better than to flout them.

"My, but you're a tricksome one, Tomas," said Oriols. He'd taken off his helmet and set it by the log he was sitting on. For all its supposed properties, the Helm Volitant looked ordinary enough, a dull thing of iron and black feathers – two of them, Tomas noted, a deep golden shade. The knight himself, however… His hair was a thornbush and scars crisscrossed his dark round face, the evidence of many battles. Despite his wounds, he might've been considered handsome once, though the size of him belayed the notion of seduction, and thereby a chance of escape. "You're more highly strung than a fairy harp! Anyone would think you guilty."

Tomas slurped his trout – surprisingly tasty, as it happened – and wrenched his eyes from the Helm Volitant (and thought of the getting of it) to offer Oriols a smile worthy of Saint Joseph. Trust be damned! Like any man, he was loath to find himself swinging from an oak in the king's orchards. The Red Rose Knight might've offered a bribe – perhaps even the Alicorn around his neck (he could always steal it back later) – when Oriols gave a belch, blinked in surprise, and then gazed at Tomas with dreamy eyes. Tomas meant to ask what he was about when a strange tingling went across his flesh and a tightening in his breeches spoke of an unbidden (and likely noticeable) arousal.

Colour, the shade of his cloak, blossomed in his cheeks.

"What is this?" he wondered, his voice aquiver. "What foul enchantment has—?"

Before he could speak further, the Black Knight was kissing him, the both of them sinking to the sward in a clatter of loosening armour. Tomas didn't stand a chance. The bulk of the man was upon him, a Foe Irresistible. In the same spirit, the Red Rose Knight tore off the man's breastplate, unbuckled his belt and yanked down his breeches. Oriols groaned as Tomas closed his lips upon his passion. The branches sighed with rain overhead.

Cross the Amorous Ford yet drink of it not lest an unsought passion befall you.

Too late Tomas recalled the words of Hellawes, his mother, and realised the river they camped beside must be the ford in question. *Oh…* Long ago, it was said that the Archimago had ensorcelled the waters so that any who drank of them would find themselves overcome with a fierce and overpowering… *Ah!* Well, you need no illustration, I'm sure. The Red Rose Knight and the Black did consort most torridly until dusk settled over the forest and ushered them into sleep. Let's leave it at that.

An owl, out looking for a stray mouse,

hooted down at the pair.

"Good gracious, sirs. Get thou to a bedchamber!"

Neither Tomas nor Oriols paid it any mind.

V

In which the Red Rose Knight reaches the mountain and finds an old woman in a cave as foretold.

At dawn, Tomas hastened from the river and raced along the edge of the forest, his boots crunching through ash. Both his head and his heart spun with unsought longing, and it was hard to tear himself from the Black Knight's side, the brute snoring next to him, scarred and naked on the sward. His cock lay on his thigh like a well-fed snake, as girthsome and grim as the rest of him. As the morning stretched on, Tomas put it down to a one-night tryst, a dalliance that he'd forbear crowing about lest the outlaws thereabouts, the rascals and rogues of Broceliande, taunt him for a trollop – and not a choosy one at that.

Blasted outlaws! Why couldn't the hellions of the forest simply heed the laws of the king? You'd never catch him sneaking through the thicket in crimson leather, fine embroidery and a macaw-feathered cap, whilst helping himself to the royal coffers. Tomas hid a smirk behind a scarlet glove as he onward roved.

In truth, the enchantment of the Amorous Ford was leaving him like the dregs of last night's wine. Such spells only lasted as long as one's bladder held and the Red Rose Knight pissed out the memory of it on steaming bark and leaves as he went.

By midday, he was merely sore, both from the saddle of his missing horse and the rigours caused by his beguilement. It came as a relief to forget Sir Oriols, in the same way he'd forgotten Persant ("Persant who?" a squirrel tittered from a lofty branch, causing Tomas to curse and hurry his step). Fortunately, he'd recovered enough of his wits to ensure he hadn't left the Helm Volitant behind. Why, Oriols would probably *want* him to have it, after the affection he'd shown him. With the horn around his neck and the helmet under his arm, Tomas came at last to the foot of the Narrow Mountain.

When all was said and done, it was a stroke of luck that he'd encountered Oriols. Such providence only occurred in fairy tales, he thought, as he stood and gazed up at the pinnacle of rock before him, its summit piercing the clouds. It was said that in the dark days before the Pendragon came, when all of Logres was aflame, the elder dragons had used the mountain as an eyrie, a place for councils conducted in *wyrm tongue*, political matings and suchlike. To forestall prying eyes and glory-seeking knights, the dragons had torn at the mountain and scorched its flanks until only this monolith remained, its soaring cliffs glossy and black, its secrets guarded.

Squinting, Tomas thought he spied a cavern far, far above, but the sweeps of smoke from the charred lands around him made it hard to be certain. Regardless, he praised his wits and his good fortune, and plucked a golden feather from the plume of the purloined helm.

Up and up, Tomas sailed, twirling now and then in an updraft, his cloak a billowing bloodstain. Below, Broceliande spread out in a sea of leaves, each the shade of a season, sweeping to the spires of Camelot to the north. You'll forgive him for pulling a face here, his guts curdling once again with the same longing and resentment that filled him whenever he saw the castle, for reasons unknown to himself. He looked away to the haze of the south, the heart of the forest where the Archimago held sway. Even that was preferable.

There is no man truer than myself,
he thought to give himself comfort.
Why, I am my own creature, wild as the woodland between my boots, of which my blood makes me a part.

Nevertheless, his heart did quail as he flitted up the flank of the Narrow Mountain and came at last to the mouth of the cavern he'd spied below. Vast it was, a maw in the rock face fit to swallow the sky. Tomas might've envisioned some treasure therein, a fabulous hoard guarded by ghosts or an enchanted grotto like the Cave of Lovers where ardent giants sought out privacy on a colossal bed of stone. Or the Cave of the Wild Hunt where Herne was said to lie sleeping and only rode out to presage some catastrophe or other, leading the souls of the dead and a pack of ghostly dogs across the night sky. Or the Cave of the Black Hag in the Valley of Distress who, once bested, might grant him his heart's desire (whatever it happened to be at the time), and send him on his way to the Fortress Impenetrable, deep in the heartwood, where Hellawes had said he would learn a Truth Most Vital. There were many caves in the kingdom.

Instead, he heard the clang of steel on stone and came to rest on the lip of the cave, crouching behind a boulder. The moment his boots touched the earth, the golden feather withered in his hand, its magic exhausted. It pained him to realise he'd have to use the last feather in the plume to descend from the eyrie, but he'd have to think on that later. He fixed his eyes on the violence before him, a flurry of armour and rags.

"Foul, thieving crone!" the one in burnished silver cried, his equally burnished sword flashing. "Release the prize you've stolen and I shall spare your life. Never let it be said that Sir Yder of Tír-Mòr is unmerciful. Do the bards not sing of my honour? Give it me and live!"

"Oh, stick it up your earsgang," said the bundle of rags that the knight was haranguing, her robes seemingly part of the cavern floor, a litter of filth, scales and bones. Her hair swung, as red and gold as brass, a fierce green eye blazing through the knotted strands. To her breast, she clutched a large spherical object – no doubt the prize in question – although Tomas failed to see what was so precious about it. It looked nothing more than a melon or a gourd. Hardly worth the climb. "Leave an old woman be!"

"Unhand the egg, Le Feu ," Sir Yder returned – if it were truly he (Tomas noted that the name came with legends attached, but the scene was unfolding fast). "Such bounty falls under the law and each must be appraised for the royal battalion. Indeed, thou art wasting my time with this ludicrous side quest, forcing me to chase you through the wasteland and up this darksome mountain. The king sent me forth to seek out one called Tomas, the self-styled 'Red Rose Knight', who dwells as an outlaw in the forest. I'm to bring him to court, you

51

see. This distraction finds me explaining my purpose as if I, the White Knight, were but a character in some tale or other, and you a happy chance to explain the plot. As you well know."

So saying, the White Knight snapped up his visor, his face a ball of frustration beneath, comely, pale and red-cheeked like many of the tribes of his distant island kingdom.

"What is your purpose to me, Sir Yder, in your satin cape with your Shield Pridwen on which is depicted Mary, the Mother of God, to keep her memory always before you and which is said to dispel any enchantment? Speaking of memory..." The old woman tilted her head, pausing for a moment. Then nodded, "Aye, I've heard of you. The name Tomas, however, means naught to me."

Like the others mentioned in the fray, the name meant something to the Red Rose Knight. It was both his pride and his calling card, left on the lips of those in his dust upon the king's roads. Wasn't his fame why the knights pursued him? Stung, he had half a mind to step out from his boulder to chide the old woman. Then he recalled the reputation of Sir Yder, foremost among the knights of the Table Round, saddler of dragons, slayer of trolls and bedder of queens (or so rumour had it). And he realised that the crone was none other than Duessa Le Feu whom his mother Hellawes had bade him find, and who, besides the Enchantress, alone knew the way to the Fortress Impenetrable.

Old and forgetful. That was her counsel. *Perhaps she'll remember me yet...*

Crowning all this was the Shield Pridwen, the bright steel disc that the knight held before him, etched on its surface with the face of the Virgin, though what Yder meant to ward off from such a shabby hag as the one before him Tomas had not the faintest idea. Duessa appeared capable of giving a good scolding, no more. Ah, but what plunder the shield would make! What a valuable tool to carry into the reaches of the forest, spurning all ensorcellment. Why, with the Horn, the Helm and the Shield in his grasp, he'd surely go skipping over the fiery chasms and marauding demons that he imagined lay between him and his destination and arrive at the fabled fortress in time for tea and cake.

Tomas was thinking this, his eyes misting over, when the old woman muttered something and flung up her hands. *'Abraxas! Calumny!'* Sparks glimmered in the gloom, dancing off the knight's shield, Yder crouching behind it. The shield had done its work, it appeared, Duessa's conjury rebuffed. It only took a moment for Tomas to see that the move had been a feint, catching the White Knight off guard. Unbeknownst to Yder, the old woman had manoeuvred him with insult and argument to the very lip of the cave.

Oh, how cunning! Tomas clapped his hands. All Duessa had to do was pretend to dart forward, her emerald eye bulging as she gave a resounding shriek. Yder lost his footing on the littered rock, his sword wheeling over his head. With a cry, part shock, part profanity, the illustrious knight dropped his shield (Tomas was glad to see it crash to the ground) and tumbled from the edge of the Narrow Mountain.

VI

In which Tomas strikes a bargain.

"Desist, knave!"

Such was the old woman's cry to dissuade the Red Rose Knight from murder – not that he was contemplating it, one hand fiddling with the rope he'd found bound to a boulder and with which, he presumed, the White Knight had climbed up to the cave. Not *truly...* From the end of it, Sir Yder swung, flashing in the sunset like some glorious pendulum, the egg clutched between his couter and vambrace. Apparently satisfied with what he'd come for, Yder was making his way down, down, his gauntlets and greaves sliding over hemp. Yet it was clear that Duessa's concern had naught to do with the knight.

"A fall from the eyrie and the egg will shatter," said she, her cheeks puffing. "It's hard to place now, but I'm sure it's important. Why else would I have the damn thing? The king's wyrmery lies under the royal garrison."

"You are asking me?" Tomas said, but relented, straightening and leaving the knight to his descent – and to fight another day. Tomas might be a thief; it wasn't in him to kill. Not unless it was necessary, anyway. And killing a knight was a grievous crime, one that reminded him he was in enough trouble as it was and should seek his mother's protection swiftly. "You're the one hiding a dragon's egg."

The old woman nodded as if reminded of something. Tomas, for his part, was weighing up the worth of such an item, to sell to the Archimago perhaps, or to ransom to the king. A shame that Yder had retrieved it, in truth. Unlike the Wyrm of the Barrow, which lived fearsome and free, now the beast would hatch and serve as a mount for some knight or other, a pawn in Arthur's wars. He'd heard that dragons had been bred for such a purpose, long ago in the mists of Time.

"Dragons shouldn't be servants," Duessa said as if reading his thoughts, a filthy fingernail stabbing out. "Old

Scaw would attest to that, after finding herself bound with reins and a bit, and she fled the king's vanguard entirely. It's Fay business and no good can come of it. Now away with ye, whoever you are. Away with your plunder and your crimson cap. I must devise a route to the egg's recovery."

"Would I at leisure to heed you," Tomas said (and he meant it; he'd much prefer to climb out of this hole and never once look back). "My mother, the Enchantress Hellawes, sent me hence to beg of you aid."

"Hellawho?"

"They call me the Red Rose Knight," Tomas said to her shrouded face and glaring eye as the old woman drew closer, scratching her head. "I seek a road to the Fortress Impenetrable." He refrained from giving her a bow. "I was told you could show me the way."

"A knight, you say?"

"After a fashion."

"Your name sounds familiar, as though these very walls echo with it."

Well they might, Tomas supposed, *considering the White Knight spoke of me mere minutes ago, along with the risk I present should you assist me.* But he neglected to tell her that.

"There's naught but high black walls and sorcery down there," Duessa went on, and made a sound of sucking her gums. Then she drew herself to her full height, which wasn't much to speak of, and regarded him through her hair for a moment. "Long has it been since I strayed into the lands of the Archimago, not since I was in the service of the king myself. Still, it's my feet that will remember, rather than my eye."

"You're saying you'll help me?"

Duessa shook her grizzled head. "Nay. I'm saying that you'll help *me*. I'm old and my wits are not what they were. Nor is my strength, which many say was formidable. Retrieve the egg from the White Knight. In return, I'll lead you to the walls of your fortress, benighted as it is."

Tomas, who fancied the egg, yet the truth more so, took a moment to consider. A thief he was, a dandy and a rogue. Yet his word was still his bond. In his mind, Hellawes rolled her eyes.

How else was he to come to her side? How else to learn a Truth Most Vital? What did the Bear King want with him?

"Very well," said he. "Then we'd best make haste. Sir Yder is nearing the treetops."

"Oh, I'll never manage such a climb," the old woman said, scowling at him for his thoughtlessness. "If only I could remember the way down the mountain. Wasn't there a hidden stair? I'm certain there was. I used to descend all the time."

Duessa rolled her shoulders, vexed by her forgetting, and looked smaller and shabbier than ever before. Tomas was doubtful she'd prove of help after all, but a promise was a promise. With a smidge of pity and a touch of regret, he lowered his shield and brandished the Helm Volitant, the last golden feather protruding from its plume.

"Say no more, my lady."

VII

In which the Red Rose Knight pursues a knight, whilst he himself is pursued by knights.

Once alighted, the feather wilting in his hand, Tomas and the old woman commenced the chase for the stolen egg. The White Knight hadn't enjoyed much of a head start, yet he soon made his way to a charger tethered at the southern fringe of Broceliande and galloped off in pursuit of the one who was watching from atop a hillock a mile or so behind him.

Although Tomas mourned the loss of

Jorget, his horse, it was fortunate that Sir Yder was travelling the same way that he meant to go, plunging further into the forest in search of the heartwood and, hopefully, the truth. Tomas could guess what his father, the old shepherd, who'd thought him both wanton and bitter, would have said about his predicament. Why couldn't he have become a squire to some duke in Camelot? Why had he chosen such a wayward life? He pictured the old man, his head bowed where Tomas tended to hold his chin aloft, his hair fair where Tomas's was dark, and his wants fulfilled by his cottage, his pigs and his vegetable patch whereas Tomas—

"What now, half-blood?"

The old woman, Duessa Le Feu, was tugging on his cloak. Tutting, she drew his gaze to the landscape behind him, which the wise called the Barrens or the Land Laid Waste, a plain of scrub, ash and broken rock, blasted by dragons, ill fortune and dolorous strokes. Indeed, it was the ash that betrayed his continuing pursuit, two spindles of dust on the road below and the riders who caused it, the flash of armour in the distance, blue and black. Both Persant and Oriols had sworn to find him, presumably to bring him to justice in Arthur's court, followed by the swing of a headsman's axe – a quest that could only be spurred by the fact of the items he'd pilfered, the Alicorn and the Helm Volitant (not to mention the Shield Pridwen and the amount of their time he'd wasted). He had no intention of letting them succeed.

You shan't catch me, kind sirs...

Well, the helmet was no longer of use to him, plucked of golden feathers as it was. He'd never much liked the fashions of knights, with their heads and limbs encased in metal, and a constant requirement for polish and oil. He preferred to clad himself in supple leather and hose that he could peel in an instant and in which he could keep his extremities loose. All the same, the sight of the knights troubled him. When he kicked the helmet down the blackened slope, he did so with some feeling. Why couldn't they just leave him alone?

"Fuck," he said to the crone at his side. "This is unfortunate. They'll be upon us come dawn. We must away at once."

A snake, slithering that way in the

vain hope of birds, said, "Oh, false knight. Thief is no name for the one who steals, but for the one who is caught. Surrender and learn your fate."

"Would that I were merely a man," Tomas spat, and shuddered. "Then the beasts of Broceliande might finally stick a cork in it."

"Broceliande?" said Duessa. "Where the devil is that?"

But Tomas hooked his arm through hers and was urging the old woman down the hill, his cape and her hair red in the wind.

For a day and a night, Tomas went after the White Knight, and the Blue and the

Black went after the Red. Adventuring was slow with the hag by his side, Duessa huffing and cursing through the briar, past the Hedged Manor where Brinol once lived, who'd hated knights with a passion until Sir Galehaut chopped off his head. The grand building was reduced to ruin and strangled by creepers and weeds.

Then past the Cursed Chapel and its Silent Guardian, some damsel screaming within. Tomas decided to ignore her when the old woman suspected the matter was a trap of some kind. And on through the fog and the rain to the Restful Hermitage where the both of them sought shelter and supped pleasant soup, and heard a tale about the Archimago from the monks within, the much feared warlock beguiling three of their chapter to serve as slaves in his fortress. And on, praise God, past the Thrice Struck Tree, their boots crunching through shards under its gnarled and ancient boughs. And on through the shadow of the Tower of Marvels (or *La Tor des Mervelles*) which Duke Ganor was said to have built at the behest of Saint Joseph of Arimathea upon the bodies of heathens who refused to convert to Christianity, which was nice.

At a signpost for the Desolate Forest, which some called the Forest of No Return and some called the Forest of Shadows and still others the Forest of Misadventure, Tomas came to a halt and informed Duessa that the crossroads presented a last chance to turn back to the woodland proper. In return, the old woman shook her head. She told him they were drawing close to the darkling heartwood and the walls of the Fortress Impenetrable – then reminded him he'd soon find himself lost in the bramble-bound maze without her assistance.

Ahead lay a great hedge, she explained, built from the bones of the giant Gargamelle and enclosing the wilder reaches of the wood where the Archimago held sway – that dealer with devils, malefactors and conspiring queens. Indeed, to pass through the Gate of the Skull was to leave Arthur's lands entirely. The Bear King himself dared not venture there, Duessa told him, wary of setting one blessed toe in the borderlands. Then she spat. In fact, she spat whenever she mentioned Arthur's name, one of her more belligerent habits, and which had caused Tomas to warm to her regardless.

This was where they found Sir Yder come dusk on the second day. Presumably, the White Knight had heard the tales too and stolen a moment to consider, perhaps wondering if the rascal he sought was bold enough to keep a hideout in such a place or whether he kept his thievery to less menacing parts.

Tomas could've enlightened the man as he watched him through the thicket, Yder chiding his reluctant horse (though no mortal was privy to the speech of beasts, luckily for them), building a fire, and then peeling off his breastplate and undershirt to wash his downy and

73

well-muscled chest in a nearby brook. In the half-light, the knight's pectorals looked like ripe, creamy fruit, his stomach as flat as the shield upon Tomas's back. It was this that inspired the Red Rose Knight, a willowy creature himself (and many said passing fair), to set about his plan, fancying he might deceive the surely-guileless paladin as the sun sank behind the hills, and unburden him of the egg. Soon enough, Yder idled beside a crackling fire, his shoulders against the towering barrier of bones of which Duessa had spoken.

In the brush, a sibilant discussion was drawing to an end.

"A 'bedder of queens', I heard," Tomas was saying, peering down at the hunched figure before him, her bulbous eye unconvinced. "As lusty as any knight! What with my willowy limbs and general comeliness, I'm sure I can provide a fitting distraction. Can you not sprinkle a modest glamour upon me, hag, to better lubricate my design? For I mean to recover your egg this very night."

Duessa sighed. Long suffering or no, he could feel her surrendering through her veil of hair. Still, she smacked her gums at him.

"Very well. But for heaven's sake, stop calling me a 'hag'. Bloody rude, it is."

"Oh, I… I meant no offense."

"Long have I lived. I was old when first I bowed to the service of the king – a matter I came to regret, with lechery in Arthur's heart and the darkest future ahead for my kind. For a while, we were as one, and I bound to the Pendragon's cause. Oh, how the two of us rode—"

"I'm sure," Tomas said, pulling a face. It was clear that Duessa was addled and her tale highly unlikely. "And I can barely wait to hear it. But another minute and our quarry will be asleep."

So it was that Sir Yder of Tír-Mòr found himself graced by the presence of Queen Belisent of Morbihan on the cusp of that long ago evening.

VIII

In which the White Knight finds himself graced by the presence of Queen Belisent of Morbihan.

"Who goes there?"

In the flickering light of the fire, a drowsy Sir Yder leapt to his feet, his sword a bright silver tongue in his hand. The blade sank to the earth as he drank in the beauty before him, a vision of ivory shoulders above the bodice of her long red dress, her locks curled on her shoulders like a portrait in some Camelot hall. And her magical shield and horn left in the thicket with the strange old woman, Duessa Le Feu, who'd agreed to becharm Tomas and thus granted him his splendid appearance.

"Kind sir," said Tomas, speaking through the veil transfigured from his cap, all feathery, crimson and sheer. In the deepening dusk, his voice rang out like orchestral bells against the loom of the bone wall, gay in a dismal place. "It is Queen Belisent of Morbihan, locked in a tower this past year by the Archimago and wandering ever since, lost in the forest. Would you share wine and give us comfort? 'Tis growing dark and it's said there are ravaging wolves hereabouts."

Somewhere behind him, the old woman attempted a howl. It sounded more like a bludgeoned crow.

Sir Yder, who had heard wolves and once wrestled with the fearsome Gorlagon, a king whose wife used a magic wand to turn him into the beast in question, cocked his head, frowning.

"Your highness, I drink not," said he. "For I am sworn not only to the king, but to Our Lord Jesus. And He would think poorly of me for succumbing to temptation."

"Oh," Queen Belisent returned, a hand to her breast. "Did Our Lord not sup Himself though? One read He was quite the vintner."

"'Twas not to make merry, my lady." The White Knight laughed, somewhat airily. "For was He not taken from that place and hung at Golgotha, perishing so that mortals might live? My abstinence is in light of His sacrifice."

Behind the mask of Queen Belisent, Tomas rolled his eyes. This was proving harder than foreseen and he was growing bored, which was oft a dangerous occurrence.

"Well, then forget Calvary and refer to Chivalry, sir, which Arthur demands of all his knights." The Queen gave her most queenly smile, her lashes aflutter. "Would you refuse a damsel in distress – and a royal one at that? Come, let us warm ourselves by your fire."

Grudgingly, the White Knight sheathed his sword and swept out his long satin cloak to shew his unexpected visitor to a spot beside the fire. There, a few feet beyond the reach of the flames, the Queen spied Yder's saddlebags and the egg resting amongst them, his steed grazing nearby.

Oh, how guileless the knight to keep it exposed in these parts, Tomas thought. *Let me but whisper a little longer, and rub him perchance, and seduce. When he sleeps, sinful and smiling, I shall away with my prize.*

With this in mind, Queen Belisent drew close to Yder as she passed, one lilywhite hand stroking his chest, so downy, creamy and well-muscled beneath his undershirt. Like fruit, truly.

"Thou art our champion, sir. Name the price of your kindness and we shall gladly pay it."

The Queen closed her eyes and tipped her head in preparation for a kiss, and hence did not see the knight blush, his cheeks turning as scarlet as her dress.

"Only Satan himself would ask reward for such welcome," said Yder, and gently pushed her away. "Your highness, I beg you. Regard me as one would regard a priest. For I'm not one for congress with imperilled ladies, lost in the woods or otherwise."

Belisent laughed, as lightly as possible, but failed to hide a sneer.

"Then thou art unlike any knight we've encountered," said she. "Why, do they not say that your legend spans the length of Broceliande, and that some of that length has been shared with the queens in the lands hereabouts? Alas, is there no truth to be found in tales at all?"

By now, the knight was aflame. "My dear lady—"

"Oh, my dear Yder. You ask us to test you most sorely!"

"My lady!"

"Hush. Fear not, champion. They say a surplus of virtue can prove a poison. Allow us to suck it out!"

All this played out in an instant, as Queen Belisent of Morbihan spooled herself in along the knight's arm and close to his chest again, one hand slipping to his groin. And then, to Yder's alarm, she dropped to her knees in a billow of crimson, her mouth pressing for the bulge in his breeches – soft yet, she found. Tomas, in his beauteous guise, was well accustomed to the bold words of knights and how most of their deeds rarely matched them, including Arthur himself. No degree of sermons and denial was about to dissuade him.

It was then that fortune intervened, and in her most ill aspect at that, for Duessa gave a squawk in the thicket, a crow throttled by a vine. Forewarned, Tomas unhanded the White Knight and sprang to his feet, turning to face the old woman in question, her eye and her hair wild as she was thrust forth without ceremony from the bushes where she'd hid. Tomas's heart sank as he took in the ones who clutched her, a gauntlet on either spindly arm.

Lucifer's scrotum!

It was Persant the Blue Knight and Oriols the Black, having caught up with him at last.

IX

In which the Red Rose Knight is captured and a mishap occurs.

Circled by knights, Tomas unsheathed his sword. It was futile, of course; he'd always relied on cunning rather than on combat and those of the Table Round had been chosen for their skill. How he rankled at capture! Restraint of any kind was torture to him (he'd once allowed a blacksmith to tie him up for a game of 'Ride the Raider', but even that had proved discomforting, not to mention the chafing). At his side, Duessa muttered curses and the odd question, like where they were and who were their assailants. She appeared to have forgotten about the egg entirely.

Sir Persant of Inde said, "The Red Rose Knight at last. Why, I knew you smacked of villainy the moment I laid eyes on you!"

"That's not all you laid on me, sir," Tomas retorted.

It was a little awkward, truth be told. The Blue Knight blushed, but he was grinning too.

"I swore you'd never escape me," Oriols of Lis cut in, his big dark face a map of scars. "Should've yielded when you had the chance and spared us this merry dance."

"Yield I did," said Tomas, waving his sword. "Did you not take me over a fallen tree on the banks of the Amorous Ford?"

Oriols grunted. What was it to him? If Tomas meant to shame his pursuers, or curry favour due to their prior affection, he was wasting his time. In those days, knights were *knights,* you understand, manly, fierce and given to duty to such a degree that humble concerns were beneath them. Like decency, for example.

"Varlet, I took you for a queen…" Sir Yder was staring at Tomas, all roguish and red in his cloak and cap, his macaw feather somewhat bent. On the knight's arm, the Shield Pridwen, recovered from the old woman in the scrub and handed him by Persant. With one sweep of it, Yder had dispelled Duessa's glamour, leaving only an unshaven, ragged and road-besmirched wretch reflected in its shimmering surface – a comely one, nonetheless. Tomas fancied the knight looked a little disappointed. "No doubt you were in league with this hag, scheming to steal treasure from the king."

Yder brandished the dragon egg, smooth as stone and the colour of a Lodainn dawn.

"Stop calling me that," Duessa hissed.

"How you knights prattle so," said the Red Rose Knight and presented them with his most impudent grin. "For reasons unfathomable, the three of you have hounded me through Broceliande, stirring up wyrms and enchantments and driving me into the heartwood. Unhand me at once! Your king has no authority here."

"I'll have my horn returned from thee!" Sir Persant cried.

"Where is my helmet, thief?" Sir Oriols demanded.

A scuffle ensued in the shadow of the bone wall where it was said Gargamelle fell, the famed lady giant who'd served the Bear King for a hundred years (Time held less meaning in those days) and helped to raise the walls of Camelot itself. Shoving Duessa to the ground and out of harm's way, Tomas wheeled and spun, his blade clanging on armour inlaid with pearl, meeting the thrust of the Blue Knight. There was scant time to get away, a fact brought home to him as Oriols grabbed his mace, the heavy spiked end of it aimed at his knees.

Dancing on air, Tomas leapt to evade its swing and kicked himself off the holy face of the Shield Pridwen, the White Knight crouching behind it. Surprised by his acrobatics, Sir Yder went stumbling backwards, his boots chasing embers from the fire. With a yelp, he dropped the shield with the sound of a Cathay gong and tumbled onto his rump in the heather. The egg went flying from his hand.

Crack!

All the knights heard it, the Blue, the Black, the White and the Red. As the echoes faded, the battle was forgotten, all four of them turning to face the spot where the egg had fallen, lying against a rock. Even in the dimming wood, the fracture was apparent, zigzagging down its otherwise rosy and untouched shell.

"Stop this madness at once," Sir Yder said, his polished shoulders falling as he took in the egg, marking that it was still intact. Then he struggled up from the ground. "The king has summoned you to court, knave. Would you refuse your destiny? Another mishap like that and we'll all face the axe."

"Tell me what the Royal Lecher wants with me," Tomas replied. "Then I might con—"

It was then a great bellow swallowed his words, shaking the trees and the bone wall above. While they bickered, the old woman had crawled to the spot where the egg had fallen and now stood cradling it in her arms. It might've been a touching sight, Duessa's concern for the egg – it was the fury in her eye that arrested them. Flames leapt in the bulging orb, green giving way to red. When she spoke, smoke came coiling from her nostrils and between her teeth. Her hair was wreathing in a strange fashion and her shoulders were rippling under her rags, as if something much larger and more dangerous than an addled hag was seeking its way out, like a wolf waking up in a hunter's sack.

"You hare-brained churls! You vainglorious cunts!" Around her feet, Tomas noticed the sward blacken and crisp, scorched by some untold heat. "Lay one finger on my egg again and all that shall return to Camelot is a curious rain of charred bones and ash."

But that was not the worst of it.

At that moment, a thunderous wind went travelling through the trees, rattling the hedge of bones and the ground under their feet. The howl of it was enough to deafen Tomas to Duessa, and even the old woman spun – shrunken yet smouldering, a hag once more – at the interruption. To his dismay, Tomas spied a billowing cloud come seething through the heartwood and the forest all around, encircling him, the hag and the three knights in a darkness deeper than night.

It was a darkness that spoke.

"Those who enter my realm must pay the toll," a resounding voice advised them from the air. "Thank you kindly for bringing me these offerings, Red Rose Knight. You may walk through the gate unharmed and thence to the walls of my fortress."

It seemed to Tomas that the tenebrous cloud was an immense cloak, trailing shadow and hooded. In its depths, he made out a gaunt and pallid face, and the sketch of a beard. And eyes like stars, pinpricks of malice in the brume.

"Wait, foul sorcerer!" cried the Red Rose Knight, for who else could it be but the Archimago who was said to hold sway in those parts? "I was summoned hence by Hellawes, my mother, and ride forth to learn a Truth Most Vital. Will you not parley with me?"

There was laughter, wicked in the dark, and a tremendous blast of wind.

When the shadow passed, the Archimago was gone.

The three knights had gone with him.

X

In which Tomas comes at last to the Fortress Impenetrable, that is sometimes called the Castle of Tears or the Castle of the Most Ill Adventure or the Castle Without A Name.

No more than a mile into the heartwood, through the yawning skull of the giant and over a bridge of glass, and Tomas came at last to the Fortress Impenetrable. Gone were the sturdy oaks, the gentle glades and the babbling brooks, the golden shafts that bejewelled Broceliande, the great Forest of Enchantment that bound Arthur's realm. Instead, all here was thorn, a briar so thick it wreathed the lowest branches of the trees, each one black, dripping and slick. Where there was no road – and there was only one – there was bubbling bog. Who knew what lurked in the mist? A darksome noise made Tomas wonder if this were perchance the Shrieking Marsh where he'd heard that adventurers were plagued by quicksand, cannibal fish, boiling waters, murderous birds, and an occasional heart-stopping wail from those who'd perished here, whose ghosts could never leave. Was that what had happened to the kidnapped monks?

"Turn back, fool," a passing bat said, flitting between the boughs overhead, black against black. "You walk where saints fear to tread. And you, briar knight, are no – *eep!"*

Tomas was all out of patience and had thrown a stone at it.

"Hark!" said he. "We have come to the fortress."

At first, Tomas imagined he was peering down the same endless tunnel of darkness, the caliginous throat that led into the forest. As they drew closer, it became clear that the darkness was solid, a colossal barrier of smooth black stone that stretched up to the starless sky. Up there, Tomas made out larger bats, flapping around the high turrets, knives against the coalsmoke clouds. It was dark, but he judged the height of the edifice at five hundred feet or more. On either side, the wall marched off into gloom, clawed at by bramble and marsh. Nor could he see a portcullis before him, no sign of any door.

"Hardly surprising for a Fortress Impenetrable," Duessa said when he remarked upon it. "You'll never survive a climb up there. The brick is sheer as glass."

Tomas shuddered, for this was the place his mother had summoned him, to the very heart of evil in the forest. And he wondered. What was the meaning of it? When all was said and done, was a Truth Most Vital so appealing? He knew of knights who'd gone after questing beasts never to return and others who'd gone in search of magical cups and never come back the same.

"Shit," said Tomas. Pouting, he regarded

the Alicorn around his neck and the Shield Pridwen on his arm. "If only I'd kept a feather from the Helm Volitant. I'd alight on those ramparts in no time."

"Well, perhaps you should knock," the old woman told him. "Whatever you decide, good luck with it! I've upheld my side of the bargain and my journey ends here." Cradled in her arms, she pressed the egg closer to her bosom, but there was kindness in her large green eye. "I must find a fitting place to leave the egg so it can make its way in the world. That's the way it is with wyrms. We barely made each other's acquaintance, Tomas, but I hope you don't fall foul of the Archimago, who'll doubtless flay you alive and use your skull as a drinking vessel."

Tomas, who found this rather specific, cocked his head as Duessa turned to leave.

"The egg is your own, is it not? I saw you by the bone wall with the knights. You were about to explode."

It hadn't escaped him that even now his pursuers might be suffering the fate that Duessa described, not that it was any of his business. Not that he winced at the thought. Another shriek came echoing through the trees.

"Perhaps," she said. "It seems there's been quite a forgetting. Aye, a forgetting since I left the service of the king and all my pretty chains. It was he who'd have my egg from me and press my spawn to the same cruel duty, pitched against a thousand poisoned lances, the devilry of Morgause and worst of all, our own kind." The old woman shook her head, a rag of sorrow and defiance. "Good luck, Red Rose Knight! Think of me should you live to tell of it, and don't wind up with your head on a flagpole or with your balls nailed to the ground. One of us, at least, should remember."

Tutting, Duessa moved away, shuffling up the darkened road.

"Old woman," Tomas told her. "*Now* is the time for remembering, for I would press you once more for aid."

So saying, the Red Rose Knight brought the Alicorn to his lips, which Sir Persant claimed had once belonged to a unicorn and which he'd procured in distant Ctesiphon. The horn held the power of 'beastly summoning', or so he'd said, calling any beast who heard it to the bearer's aid – including, he supposed, forgetful old women.

As the sweetest music rang out through the briar (it was the sound of angel's weeping, if you want an example), and the mist and the murk recoiled, the one called Duessa Le Feu (who in her younger days had gone by the name Pennydrake, the same as the legendary mount of King Arthur himself) rippled and seethed, her wings unfolding in a mess of broken trees. Horns and scales writhed in the gloom, lengthening and swelling.

Christ's crap! Tomas had seen her before, he realised then. Here was the Wyrm of the Barrow, gigantic, fabulous and fierce, red plated in a way he couldn't help but admire. Looking up into eyes as golden as the sun, as large as cartwheels, he uttered a command to her smouldering maw.

XI

In which Tomas learns a Truth Most Vital.

Down a corridor as dark as night went the Red Rose Knight. He'd said farewell to the dragon on the battlements, releasing Duessa to her business in the forest, whatever wyrms liked to do with their eggs (no doubt to hide them from knights) and watched her swoop off over the treetops, each branch clawing at the sky. Thinking of knights, he quailed at the thought of what the Archimago had done with his pursuers and the more chill halls he passed though, the more he wished he'd bound the old woman – or the beast – to his cause. But a bargain was a bargain and a creature of her size would barely fit down here, and likely brought the fortress down upon his head.

In a chamber of shrouded, threadbare furniture, a mirror spoke to him, calling out his name. In another, a baby wailed in a giant crib, one chubby pink hand the size of the trees outside. In a web-draped ballroom, a host of skeletons danced, their bones clacking under motheaten robes as they turned about the tiled floor. Sword held high, peering over his shield, Tomas swore under his breath at each horror until he reached the throne room.

"Ah, welcome!" the echoes boomed from the vaults of the great hall where a single shaft of sunlight speared from a window high above. "Welcome, Red Rose Knight, to the hour of your destiny."

Eyes wide, Tomas drank in the sight before him. The chamber was vast, the middle of it taken up by a long wooden table, its length laden with a feast. Piles of fruit, sweetmeats and steaming hogs hardly left room for the tablecloth, and he noticed how a trio of monks went back and forth (doubtless the ones abducted from the Restful Hermitage and enslaved here by sorcery), bringing jugs and platters for the guests, who filled the table from end to end although Tomas could neither see nor hear them. All he could see was a chicken leg dancing in the air, teeth marks appearing in white flesh. Knives and forks floated on the

air, bearing potatoes and peas. He saw
a bunch of grapes dangling on nothing,
each one popping into some unseen
mouth. Here and there, goblets tipped
back and forth, spilling wine into ghostly,
silent throats.

At the head of the table, in an ornate,
highbacked chair, sat the Archimago. The
Host of the Invisible Feast was robed all
in black and bearded. Warlocks tended
to cleave to a certain fashion and Tomas
wasn't surprised to see him thus garbed
nor to find him here, no more than he
was the theatrical greeting. At least the
Archimago hadn't said it was the hour of
his doom.

"This is rather overblown," said
Tomas, coming to the other end of the
table. "I came not on a rescue mission

nor to challenge some felonious mage. It was my mother, Hellawes, who summoned me hence to learn a Truth Most Vital. Forgive me, my lord, but I'm assuming this bears something in common. Out with it, warlock, or I'll ride off into the wood and seek an adventure of greater interest, and more pecuniary promise."

So saying, Tomas affected a yawn, although his heart did thunder.

"Three knights hunted you in the forest," the Archimago replied, rising from his seat in a billow of smoke, another nod at dramatics. "The Blue, the Black and the White. And you would know the why of it, isn't that so?"

"Indeed, I—"

His words dried up in his throat as the

Archimago waved a typically long sleeve at one wall of the chamber. Besides the garish tapestries, Tomas saw what else was hanging there. Bound in chains, naked to a man, he spied Sir Persant of Inde, Sir Oriols of Lis and Sir Yder of Tír-Mòr suspended upside down against the blackened stone. On another day, Tomas might've tarried to admire their physiques, chiselled from the work of serving the king, and the fine cocks that dangled to their bellies (two of which he'd had the pleasure of), but to focus on that in his predicament was unwise, not to mention inappropriate, and truly nothing to do with the story. Instead, in the shaft of sunlight falling from on high, he took in the piles of armour and weapons beneath them, a breastplate enamelled and inlaid with pearl, a large black mace and a shining white helm. He looked up at their empty eyes, their minds beguiled by enchantment.

An offering. That's what the Archimago had called the knights in the forest. *But an offering to whom?*

To that end, he asked, "What is the meaning of this?"

"Why," the Archimago said, and chuckled. "This is where we shall take our revenge, my boy. Three knights pursued you through Broceliande, despatched by Arthur the king. And three heads you shall carry back to him in answer for his summons. And his crime."

Tomas stepped around the table, fearful of the warlock yet ever more curious.

"The king… I know not why he seeks me. And his crime could be one of hundreds. Speak, mage, and spare me this game."

"Ah, but 'tis one and the same," the Archimago told him. "Upon his last breath, an old shepherd in the forest – O' Lincoln was his name – commanded a letter sent to the king to appraise him of the matter. Did you imagine an enchantress as fair as Hellawes would bed with a simple pig herder, Tomas? Nay, she once lay with the king himself on one of his many wanderings, who thought her a humble damsel in a tower and so grateful for rescue."

"My…mother?"

Such things were hardly beyond her. But the *king?*

"Aye. Afterwards, when she found herself with child, Hellawes went to Camelot to beg Arthur for aid. Instead, he turned her away from court, for what did he care for wayward damsels? How many had he swived in the woods? Oh, he was not yet counselled on congress with fairies nor the folly of his spurning. Long lived and biding her time, your mother spirited her get away into Broceliande. In return for a cottage, healthy livestock and a vegetable patch, the old shepherd agreed to raise you as his own."

Tomas shook his head. "Say it isn't so!"

All the same, he could not shake off the memory of his mother's bitterness, the many unkind names she'd called the king over the years, from 'bedswerver' to 'lecher' to 'Pin-dick-dragon'. Though he hated the words he was hearing, the sense of them was undeniable, cooling his otherworldly blood.

"The Fay look to their own, Tomas," said the warlock with a touch of rue. "It was in your blood to stay wild. Wild and in our sorcerous service!"

Tomas staggered backwards, falling to one knee. In his mind, he recalled Persant, begging him not to flee. Then Oriols, who claimed that his business with the Red Rose Knight should only fall from the king's lips. And Yder, the White Knight himself, seeking him out in the forest… It occurred to Tomas then that the Bear King would never have sent the best of his champions in pursuit of a common thief, let alone to bring him to court. More than likely, Arthur would've sent some assassin to lop off his head and kick it into the briar, if enough gold had gone missing from his carriages, that was. In those days, Camelot hardly wanted for gold. Like gold, the knowledge weighed upon him, glittering, glorious and grim, a destiny that promised much yet shattered all he had known.

Now I know why the old shepherd lamented of my ways, thought Tomas, dazed and trembling on the floor. *But I remain true to myself, and my own creature, wild as the woodland between my boots, of which my blood makes me a part.*

To the Archimago, he said, "Oh, a Truth Most Vital comes with a sting. Even where I thought I was cherished I was not. But I serve no one, warlock. Least of all thee."

"Alas," said the Archimago, "thou art wrong. For cherished you are, my son. Look upon your mother, Hellawes, and do my bidding!"

With this, Tomas looked up through his tears to see the Archimago wrench at his beard and reveal the beauteous face beneath – none other than that of his mother's, the Enchantress Hellawes, who had deceived him in the Clearing of the Fairy Fountain and lured him to the Fortress Impenetrable. And all, it appeared, to exact her revenge.

"Be not alarmed," said Hellawes. "Did I not tell you that the Archimago and I came to a 'mutual accord'? Aye, here you find it in false hair and shadow. How else should I have hidden myself these years since my spurning, but in the darkling heartwood and behind the blackest walls? Long have I waited for you to grow to manhood, Tomas, and grant me the tool to take my vengeance on the cunt-king of Camelot."

"Mother," said Tomas, and winced for she had never taken to the courtly tongue. "That isn't very nice."

"Three knightly heads shall you bear to the king," Hellawes went on. "Along with a curse I shall place on your blade. When you kneel before Arthur to lament the death of these of the Table Round, a hand he shall place on your shoulder and draw you into his embrace. Then shall you plunge your sword through his heart and end the Pendragon tyranny!"

"Oh, mother," said Tomas, and climbed to his feet. "That sounds like asking for trouble."

"You would defy me, Tomas? The very branch that bore you?"

Shadows boiled around her highbacked chair. Could she see the struggle in his heart?

"It strikes me, mother, upon hearing this Truth, that I stand with a boot in both worlds. One placed in the land of the Fay and one in Arthur's realm. Who then should I serve?"

Hellawes cried out, her fury ringing off stone. She was too late to prevent the Red Rose Knight from leaping for the wall, his blade striking the pulley of chains that held the knights aloft. In a deafening clatter, Persant, Oriols and Yder fell to the floor among their armour and weapons, which they were pulling on even as the echoes faded.

"Fool! Bastard! Traitor!"

Pale hands high, the Enchantress shrieked and flung her sorcery against the knights, the Blue, the Black and the White, all ready and armed with sword and mace, if not wearing any braies. And Tomas, the Red, who turned to face her as she hissed foul curses and summoned the vampire bats down from the vaults, and hollered for the ogres lurking in the dungeons, and cried for the flagstones to spin under their boots and for the invisible guests to rise from the table, a wall of knives and forks aloft on the air, and all come rushing towards them.

"Oh, mother," said Tomas. "I made no promises."

Then the Red Rose Knight raised the Shield Pridwen, upon the face of which was etched that of Mary, the Mother of God, to keep her memory always before the bearer and which was said to dispel any enchantment. Angled to reflect the shaft of sunlight falling through the window above, Tomas repelled the spells of Hellawes the Enchantress and heard her receding scream as a cloud of billowing black smoke enveloped the chamber and she vanished from the Fortress Impenetrable.

XII

*In which the Red Rose Knight returns to
the Forest of Enchantment and makes his
one and only promise.*

It befell in the days of Arthur Pendragon,
when he was king of all England, and
so reigned, that there lived a thief and
a lover of men called Tomas, the Red
Rose Knight. Now, kind reader, you
have heard this tale, which does not
rest in the *Annales Cambriae* or the
Vita Merlini, nor in any surviving ancient
texts. Many years after this account,
an English writer by the name of

Richard Johnson will come to remember Tom O'Lincoln, the Red Rose Knight, and publish a romance in two parts in 1599 and 1607 respectively, but that's hardly of consequence now. And the Victorians preferred to forget him entirely, bothersome as he was. 'Borrowed Arthuriana' some called it.

How he strode, our errant knight, our fabled far-from-champion in his red leather armour, his cloak and macaw-feathered cap. Raven haired and spark-eyed, he emerged at last from the heartwood and climbed to a bluff overlooking the great Forest of Enchantment that in those days was called Broceliande and swept as far as the eye could see. In the distance rose the shining spires of Camelot, the heart of Arthur's fabled realm, and at Tomas's side stood the three rescued knights, Sir Persant of Inde, Sir Oriols of Lis and the somewhat chagrined Sir Yder of Tír-Mòr who would later tell a rather different version of this story and bask in the glow of adoration. Tomas had given him his shield back and Persant his horn, out of sympathy if nothing else. Besides, he would not fight them.

"Come now," said Persant. "Away to Camelot and the king!"

"Away," chimed Oriols. "To take up your destiny."

"We were sent to seek an outlaw," said Yder, and clapped Tomas on the shoulder. "We return with a foundling prince."

Tomas, on hearing them, gazed to the north, over the gold-and-copper sea of the treetops. Down there, he of all people knew the dangers and mysteries that lurked in the thicket, from the Hollow Hill to the Isle of the Stag to the Church of the Deaths where the lost treasures of Atlantis were said to lie buried. Yet when he looked to the great white castle ahead of him, where the Bear King sat his throne, he discovered that resentment no longer tugged at his heart or the shadow of a nameless shame, for both in him had been answered. Nor did he find longing and when he turned to the knights, it was with an honest smile.

"Away, aye," he told them. "Away to duty and kneeling and burdensome quests. Away to a life behind high stone walls with a heavy golden circlet on my head. Broceliande remains my home."

"Then you'll not come?" Yder asked. The knights looked at him astonished, and rueful to a one.

"Forgive me, sirs," Tomas replied, for it seemed he had settled on his own Truth and voiced some prattle of his own. "For I am my own creature, wild as the woodland between my boots, of which my blood makes me a part. The only away you'll see this day is from Tomas himself!"

With a flourish, Tomas stole a breath and leapt from the bluff, his cloak a flag on the air. *Farewell.* He knew the forest like the back of his hand and was aware of a lake far below, its glittering surface shrouded by the trees, and which he was certain would break his fall. As the wind rushed in his ears and carried away the cries of his captors, Tomas prayed that the pouches of gold that were in his pockets, and moments before in theirs, wouldn't weigh him down too much. Water he could bear.

In this fashion, the knights of Camelot and a Destiny Most Unfitting were left in the dust of the Red Rose Knight.

About the Author

James Bennett is a British writer raised in Sussex and South Africa. His travels have furnished him with an abiding love of different cultures, history and mythology.

His short fiction has appeared internationally and his debut novel *Chasing Embers* was shortlisted for Best Newcomer at the British Fantasy Awards 2017.

James lives in Spain where he's currently at work on a new Fantasy novel.

Also by James Bennett

Chasing Embers

Raising Fire

Burning Ash

The Book of Queer Saints
Anthology

More dyslexic friendly

titles coming soon...

Ingram Content Group UK Ltd.
Milton Keynes UK
UKHW042133120323
418425UK00004B/82